ERIC CARLE
Pancakes, Pancakes!

by Eric Carle

READY-TO-READ

SIMON SPOTLIGHT

New York   London   Toronto   Sydney   New Delhi

This book was previously published with slightly different text.

SIMON SPOTLIGHT

An imprint of Simon & Schuster Children's Publishing Division
1230 Avenue of the Americas, New York, New York 10020
For information about special discounts for bulk purchases, please contact Simon & Schuster Special Sales at 1-866-506-1949 or business@simonandschuster.com.
The Simon & Schuster Speakers Bureau can bring authors to your live event. For more information or to book an event contact the Simon & Schuster Speakers Bureau at 1-866-248-3049 or visit our website at www.simonspeakers.com.
Manufactured in the United States of America 0317 LAK
10 9 8 7 6 5
Library of Congress Cataloging-in-Publication Data
Carle, Eric.
Pancakes, Pancakes! / by Eric Carle. — 1st ed.
p. cm. — (Ready-to-read)
This book was previously published with slightly different text.
Summary: By cutting and grinding the wheat for flour, Jack starts from scratch to help make his breakfast pancake.
[1. Pancakes, waffles, etc.—Fiction. 2. Cooking—Fiction.] I. Title.
PZ7.C21476Pan 2013
[E]—dc23
2012017343
ISBN 978-1-4424-7274-7 (pbk)
ISBN 978-1-4424-7275-4 (hc)
This book was previously published with slightly different text.

Kee-ke-ri-kee!

A rooster crowed.

Jack woke up and thought,

"I want a pancake."

Jack said to his mother,

"Can I have a pancake?"

"You can help me make it,"

said his mother.

"First we need some flour."

"Cut some wheat, please.
Then take it to the mill
to grind into flour."

So Jack cut the wheat.

Then he went to the miller.

Jack asked him

to grind the wheat.

First they had

to beat the grain

from the wheat.

"Now we will grind the grain
to make the flour,"
said the miller.

Jack helped the miller
to make the flour.
Then he took
the flour home.

"Can we make a pancake?"
asked Jack.

"Now we need an egg,"
said his mother.

So Jack got an egg

from the hen house.

"Can we make a pancake?"

asked Jack.

"Now we need some milk,"

said his mother.

So Jack milked the cow.

"Can we make a pancake?"
asked Jack.

"Now we need some butter,"
said his mother.

So Jack churned
some butter.

"Can we make a pancake?"
asked Jack.

"Now we need to make a fire,"
said his mother.

So Jack got some firewood.

"Can we make a pancake?"
asked Jack.

"Now we need some jam,"
said his mother.

So Jack got some

strawberry jam.

"Can we make a pancake?"
asked Jack.

"Yes!" said his mother.

So Jack and his mother

mixed everything in a bowl.

They put some butter
in a hot pan.

"Jack, now put some
batter in the pan,"
said Jack's mother.

Jack's mother

cooked the pancake.

Then she flipped it.

The pancake flew up high.

It landed in the pan.

Jack's mother put the
pancake on a plate
and gave it to Jack.
Jack said,
"Mama, I know
what to do now!"